Bright
Summaries.com

Thoughts

BY BLAISE PASCAL

BOOK ANALYSIS

Written by Natacha Cerf
Translated by Oliver Brown

Thoughts

BY BLAISE PASCAL

BLAISE PASCAL

French scientist, moralist, philosopher and theologian.

- Born in 1623 in Clairmont

- Died in 1662 in Paris

- Some of his works:

  - *The Provinciales* (1656-1657), correspondence

  - *The Art of Persuasion* (1660), a philosophical work

  - *Thoughts* (1670), set of fragments

Blaise Pascal (1623-1662) was a man of letters, a scientist and a theologian. From an early age, he distinguished himself by his extraordinary intelligence. As a teenager, he wrote a treatise on sounds, an essay on conics and, at the age of nineteen, he invented the calculating machine. In 1654, Pascal was involved in a carriage accident that made him aware of the fragility of life. The incident marked the beginning of his religious preoccupations. His Christian ideals made him give up science: he devoted himself to philosophical and religious reflection, and wrote *Les Provinciales*, eighteen letters defending the Jansenist theses.

Blaise Pascal greatly influenced the scientific method, economic theories and social sciences. He died of illness without having seen the *Pensées* published.

THOUGHTS

The work of a moralist and a theologian

- **Genre:** essay

- **Reference edition:** *Pensées*, Paris, Éditions France Loisirs, collection « Les grands écrivains choisis par l'Académie Goncourt », 1986.

- **1st edition:** 1670

- **Themes:** Christianity, happiness, politics, humanity, justice

Pascal's posthumous work published in 1670, the *Pensées* are a response to a desire to demonstrate that man can only find inner peace and true happiness by accepting to be touched by the grace of God. Man without God is miserable and finite, whereas God is all-powerful and infinite.

Politics, man and the sovereign good are the major themes addressed by the philosopher-theologian in his work. The echoes of Pascal in modernity are numerous and the topicality of his reflections permanent.

SUMMARY

SECTION 1 – THOUGHTS ON MIND AND STYLE

In the spirit of geometry, the principles are known principles on which one can only reason well. In the spirit of finesse, the principles are not easily handled and one feels them more than one sees them. It is difficult to make them felt by those who do not feel them for themselves. Their object cannot be grasped by progressive reasoning, but only in their totality. The spirit of finesse is concerned with things related to feelings, the spirit of geometry with things of reasoning.

SECTION 2 – MISERY OF MAN WITHOUT GOD

Men have sought to understand the principles of things to the point of knowing the whole with infinite pride, but a man is nothing in the infinite and cannot under stand the principles of things in totality. He stands between nothing and everything, and must recognise his limited scope. Nothingness and wholeness are found only in God, the omnipotence and seat of the reality of all things:

Old impressions, the charms of novelty, appearances, feelings and our own interest are causes of bad judgements. All this dominates reason to the point of disposing of everything: justice, happiness and the whole world. Man is therefore nothing but disguise, lies and hypocrisy; both in himself and with regard to others. He does not want to be told the truth, he avoids telling it to others; and all these dispositions, so far removed from justice and reason, have a natural root in his heart (p. 59).

The human condition consists of inconstancy, anxiety and boredom. It is an unhappy condition from which man vainly tries to escape through entertainment (gambling, war, women, etc.). Death, misery and ignorance are ignored because they are incurable and make one unhappy. Entertainment is the only thing that consoles us from our miseries.

SECTION 3 – THE NEED FOR BETTING

God puts religion in the mind by reason and in the heart by grace. He is infinitely incomprehensible because He has no relation to us, limited beings. We are unable to know if He is or what He is because an infinite chaos separates us.

We can only know God through the submission of reason. Faith is a matter of the heart and not of science. It is necessary and allows us to move away from stale pleasures to embrace honesty, faithfulness, humility and sincerity.

SECTION 4 – MEANS OF BELIEF

We have to submit ourselves ostensibly to God and wait for Him on the outside so that He can visit us on the inside. He submits our soul naturally without art or argument. All reasoning is reduced to yielding to feeling; since religion is mysterious and supernatural, it cannot submit to reason. The impossibility of proving the existence of God by reason proves nothing else than the weakness of our reason. First principles are felt and come from the heart; men who have the disposition of religion in their hearts need no more to understand that they must love God and hate only themselves. God Himself inclines to believe; no more is needed to be persuaded.

SECTION 5 – JUSTICE AND THE REASONS FOR EFFECTS

Justice should be the same for all states in the world and in all times, since it is not in customs but in natural laws. But everything changes with time, and according to the goodwill of kings and dictators. Powers are established according to the whims of the moment; therefore, there is no constancy in law and justice. Therefore, the people take the antiquity of customs as proof of their truth, which explains the falsity of their opinions. Man's actions are governed by weakness, concupiscence and power relations.

SECTION 6 – PHILOSOPHERS

Thought is great by its nature, but low by its defects: thought is easily manipulated, everything can always be proved and its opposite. Man without God is therefore in ignorance of everything and in inevitable unhappiness because he cannot be sure of any truth even though he would like to be.

Man must know his lowliness as well as his greatness and never one without the other. The search for the true good is useless, one must just reach out to the liberator.

SECTION 7 – MORALITY AND DOCTRINE

God is the true good. He wanted to make himself perfectly known to those who sincerely seek Him and hidden from those who cordially shun Him.

Man's true nature, his true good, true virtue and true religion cannot be known separately. God alone gives wisdom.

Religion teaches us that the connection between man and God was broken by a man (original sin) and then restored by Christ: Christ is the mediator making communication with God possible. The prophecies are solid proof of the existence of Jesus Christ.

Scripture, original sin and Christ absolutely prove God, doctrine and morality. Christ makes us know our misery because He is the repairer of our misery. Now we only know God well by knowing our iniquities. Therefore, without the Scripture which has only Jesus as its object, we know nothing, not even ourselves.

SECTION 8 – THE FOUNDATIONS OF THE CHRISTIAN RELIGION

We must know God and His misery, not one without the other. Men are both unworthy of God by their corruption and capable of God by their first nature. We are miserable and separated from God, but redeemed by Jesus Christ. The truth of religion is recognised in the very darkness of religion. God is partly hidden and partly uncovered, and this is useful: the darkness so that man may feel his corruption and the light so that he may hope for a remedy.

LIGHTING

BIRTH OF FAITH

In Pascal's family, everyone was a believer, with a sincere but lukewarm faith. It was not until 1646 that Pascal experienced "his first conversion" when the Deschamps brothers, called to his father's bedside for his dislocated leg, transmitted the Augustinian ideology to the family. His sister Jacqueline joined the religious community of Port-Royal in 1652, which applied the thought of Saint Augustine in its most severe and intransigent version: the clerics, theologians, scholars and laymen who lived in the convent led an extremely simple and austere life.

Pascal's 'second conversion' occurred one night in 1654 after a coma caused by a carriage accident. When he wakes up, the scholar describes a mystical experience. Pascal passionately proclaimed his new faith and devoted himself to religion for good. He went to Port-Royal for a while and embraced its cause, although he was never officially a member of the community. It was at this time that he began to work on his great project of *Apologie de la Religion Chrétienne*.

BIRTH OF A WORK

Pascal never wrote a book entitled *Pensées*. The editors presented the scattered drafts left by the author as a complete work, which is largely made up of the preparatory documents for the *Apology of the Christian Religion*: this new work built on the ruins of the *Apology* is as much theirs as Pascal's. According to the editors, the theologian himself announced a deliberately discontinuous presentation in the form of a collection of maxims (segmented units). However, it is not impossible that this announcement was actually that of the editors.

Pascal hastily scribbled his ideas on sheets of paper to escape the transience of his thoughts by freezing them. The *Pensées* are therefore a testimony to the urgency of writing, a symptom of the human drama of the horrible passage of time and of things. This recourse to the "notepad" explains the telegraphic character of the work. It is still only a sketch, a promise of a speech.

When the writer died, his relatives discovered files full of pages sewn together with thread. Themes could be derived from them, but it was not possible to conclude what the actual parts of an intended plan were. Perhaps this was just a personal method of filing. Pascal's entourage initially decided to copy the bundles identically, but in a century where disdain for disjointed forms was the norm, the text was unpublishable as is. In 1670, the decision was therefore taken to produce a selective and corrected edition: the Port-Royal edition, an overly refined version that retracted the writer's very personal syntax, his audacity, as well as certain key passages of his argument. In the 19th century , a finally complete edition of the *Pensées* was demanded. Nevertheless, although exhaustive, the modern editions remain the personal interpretations of the editors on the reconstitution of the order of the fragments. The *Pensées* are an uncertain, shifting and malleable work that can only be cast in the mould of its interpreters.

AUGUSTINISM

The influence of St. Augustine (a Christian philosopher and theologian born in 354 and died in 430) on Pascal's work is great. Pascal took over a substantial part of his dark and tragic conception of religion from the bishop. He shares the idea that original sin is the root of the irreversible corruption of the human race. Man is a puppet manipulated by three kinds of concupiscence: curiosity, pride and lust. In the face of these temptations, Augustinian morality advocates sole concern for God against the vanities of science, deep humility against the aspiration to power, and absolute abstinence as a remedy for the temptations of the flesh. True certainty is found in faith, not in reason. Pascal says no different. He defends a Christianity cast in terror and restriction that assures salvation only to a very few individuals, chosen by a lottery of divine grace. Man's predestination is tragic; indeed, no matter what he does, he has no control over his future.

READING KEYS

A THEOLOGICAL WORK

The *Pensées* bear witness to the belief system of the 17th century. Religion had an enormous hold on people's minds at the time: it imposed its laws everywhere and guided thought. The ecclesiastical authorities controlled published works and regulated censorship, and heretics were burned in the name of the one-track mind. This is a much darker Christianity than that of today, where the fear of God is central. Consequently, a rigorously historical reading of the *Pensées* is in order: the reader must avoid the pitfall of anachronisms in order not to be offended by Pascal's words and not to miss the greatness of the work.

The figure of God

From the Scriptures, Pascal retains the great, powerful and terrible God. He is a universal being capable of losing you at any moment. He is both threat of punishment and consolation. In other words, God is as much sweetness, love and charity as he is vengeance and terror. He is hidden from the eyes of reason or the soul, but not entirely: He allows Himself to be glimpsed without quite appearing. This partial concealment of God separates men into the elite and the blind masses. Those who sincerely seek Him find Him, but He remains hidden from those who do not seek Him. To desire God is therefore already to possess Him.

Original sin

Pascal delivers a tragic vision of Christianity according to which man is irreparably unhappy because he knows that he was happy and is no longer happy. The Fall imposes suffering and penance on mankind, and Christians must pay indefinitely for a crime they did not commit according to a divine justice whose principle escapes reason. The human condition is miserable because man lives with the memory of lost happiness; this is the cruelest of torments. Man's first nature is irrevocably lost and the lack of happiness impossible to fill. The work is marked by a sense of anguish and narrowness linked to man's mortal condition, which brings the *Pensées* closer to the tragic genre.

The Christ

Pascal reduces Christian doctrine to two equal and opposite powers: the corruption of nature and the redemption of Jesus Christ. Christ unites in himself human and divine nature to reconcile men with God in his divine nature. He embodies redemption. In this way, Christ teaches a twofold lesson: there is a God of whom men are worthy and a God of whom men are unworthy because of the corruption of nature. Jesus is the repairer, redeemer and liberator, who makes amends for the original sin and opens the way to salvation. Christ is also an intermediary. Communication between the finite and the infinite is impossible without a mediator; it is He who makes the reunification between God and man possible. Christ has an absolutely central place: without Him, we would know neither life nor death, neither God nor ourselves.

The need for faith

Pascal does not seek to transmit faith since it cannot be transmitted by reasoning, but to prove its necessity. Faith is a gift from God. It exceeds and contradicts reason. Belief is the abandonment of reason in favour of a superior truth that sometimes clashes with it. But if Pascal does not try to transmit faith, he nevertheless recommends a morality and a way of life that are consistent with the life of a Christian. Even the man who is not visited by God's grace can prepare himself inwardly to become a Christian by living outwardly as one. God could in this case grant His grace *in fine*. However, as an Augustinian, the thinker states that not all men will be saved.

GREATNESS AND MISERY OF MAN

The essential argument of the work is that of contrarieties, i.e. the internal contradictions of man: he is both full of greatness and full of misery. Pascal considers Christianity to be the only philosophical system that expresses these two contradictory aspects in a comprehensive way, the doctrine that accounts for everything. Before the Fall, man was close to God and dignified by Him, who placed him at the centre of creation. It is the memory of this bliss, which has been lost forever, that makes man great. Man's misery, on the other hand, is the result of original sin, which condemns him to permanent torment.

Reconciling annoyances

The complete truth is made of the union of two opposites: man is both greatness and misery. Pascal challenged the principle of non-contradiction which states that a given proposition cannot be both true and false. The error is in the incompleteness and not in the falsity of one of the two propositions. Pascal denounces the stoicism of Epictetus, who sees only the greatness of man, and the scepticism of Montaigne, who sees only his misery: "It is therefore from these imperfect lights that it happens that one, knowing the duties of man and ignoring his impotence, loses himself in presumption; and that the other, knowing impotence and not duty, falls into cowardice." (from the *Interview with M. de Sacy*, 1655) Christianity overcomes philosophies by unifying opposing theses. Incompatible truths in human doctrines are brought together by the truth of the Gospel. Moreover, man is not in the middle, but simultaneously very high and very low. Christian morality is a permanent correction which lowers proud men and raises humble men.

The thought

It is through thought that man rises above the animal kingdom. Thought makes man great. Man is both body and spirit, but the spirit infinitely exceeds the body. There is an absolute contrast between the weakness of the body and the power of the mind. Ontologically, the spirit is superior to the whole of the material universe: the spirit is infinitely larger than the whole of the universe. It is in this that man is both profoundly insignificant and supremely worthy. But if thought signals man's greatness, it is also the essential drama that makes it possible to realise the extent of his distress. Man is miserable, but great in being aware of it. The main mark of greatness, thought, is therefore still misery.

Entertainment

Entertainment is the poor response to the desire to escape misery and confirms man's unhappy condition, since if man were happy, he would not need to divert his thoughts through entertainment. Without entertainment, man sinks into boredom and then into absolute despair. This ridiculous solution only masks the problem without ever solving it and, more often than not, throws man into indignity. Play and bodily pleasures are unworthy of the greatness of his thought. Moreover, it is inherently inefficient since it has no extrinsic purpose. Pascalian amusement is comparable to Freudian repression. Both are attempts to forget painful thoughts that inevitably end in failure: the disturbing ideas always return, bringing with them many torments. Pascal wants to denounce the form of blindness that is entertainment. Apart from God, there is no escape from the anguish of emptiness. A proliferation of doing will never compensate for the lack of being.

The deceitful powers and concupiscence

The deceptive powers are everything that can lead us into error and are an obstacle to the truth. Among them, we distinguish:

- Imagination, the irreducible part of irrationality that man carries within him, which dominates the subject and suspends his senses. Because of it, man no longer masters his own inner life. Pascal seeks to give man a healthier view of reality;

- interest or self-esteem;

- custom. Man unconsciously takes local convention for universality. Habits of thought, ideologies and traditions are the customs that Pascal spoke of and that today we would call culture, as opposed to nature. It is the source of most of our convictions and certainties, the majority of which are not rooted in reason. Customs are stronger evidence for reason than experience. Pascal noted the extreme relativity of laws that vary from one place to another and change according to the times: everyone follows the customs of his country and his time. The observation of such friable truths imposes the search for a stable and universal truth.

Concupiscence, on the other hand, is a moral obstacle that has three aspects: pride, curiosity and concupiscence of the flesh.

The transience

It relates to the great philosophical and literary theme of the vanity of all things. The very nature of the human condition, a consequence of the Fall, is ephemerality. This transience of things is opposed to the divine immobility and eternity. Man is nothing but inconstancy and incoherence.

THE REASONING

The work is a lengthy argument that is entirely rhetorical. Pascal knows how to use the appropriate means to persuade his readers. The author attaches great importance to the arrangement of words and the plan, and claims a simple and natural style as opposed to the brilliance of eloquence. The writer deploys several forms of reasoning:

- inductive reasoning: reasoning which consists in starting from a particular case to deduce a general law. Example: "Whoever wishes to know the full extent of man's vanity need only consider the causes and effects of love. [...] Cleopatra's nose, if it had been shorter, would have changed the whole face of the earth."(pp. 82-83) Pascal deduces here from Cleopatra's individual charm the universal upheavals that love can cause;

- analogical reasoning: reasoning by association of ideas. From certain visible similarities between two situations, we conclude that there are other less obvious similarities. Example: "Don't let it be said that

I haven't said anything new, the arrangement of the materials is new. When we play palm, it is the same ball that we both play, but one places it better" (p. 20);

- deductive reasoning: deductive reasoning starts from a general idea, a principle, a law, to draw a particular consequence. For example, Pascal says, roughly, that evidence the denial of which constitutes a sin is indubitable; now, Christ's contemporaries who disputed the miracles were sinners; therefore, the miracles constitute indubitable evidence;

- à fortiori reasoning: reasoning by which one truth is shown to lead to another, supported by more powerful arguments. A law that is verified in a first case that is at first sight not very favourable will be verified all the more so in other, more favourable cases: "If natural things surpass [reason], what will be said of the supernatural?" (p. 127);

- reasoning by the absurd: the validity of a given hypothesis is demonstrated by the absurdity of the opposite hypothesis. Example: "If our condition were truly happy, we should not be entertained by thinking about it.";

- mathematical reasoning: argumentation in the form of absolutely and definitively indisputable scientific proof. It is a reasoning that is meant to be unstoppable: "If there were an infinite number of chances, only one of which would be for you, you would still be right to gamble one in order to have two [...]; but here there is an infinite number of infinitely happy lives to be won, a chance of gain against a finite number of chances of loss, and what you are gambling on is finite."

FOOD FOR THOUGHT

A FEW QUESTIONS TO DEEPEN YOUR REFLECTION...

- Book professionals find Pascal's work a headache to classify. How do you explain this?

- What link can be established between the Freudian theory of repression and Pascal's reflections on the unbearable idea of our death?

- Jean Mesnard sees Pascal as a precursor of contemporary existentialism. Do you agree with him?

- What difference(s) is there between Pascalian ennui and Camus' sense of the absurd?

- *A King Without Entertainment* contains quotes from Pascal. Is Jean Giono's view of the world similar to Pascal's?

- What is the influence of Saint Augustine on Pascal's *Pensées*?

- Pascal is divided between Augustinianism and Jansenism. Explain.

- Identify some aporias (unresolvable contradictions) in Pascal's argument.

- What is Pascal's relationship with scepticism (a philosophical doctrine according to which man cannot attain knowledge of the truth)?

TO GO FURTHER

REFERENCE EDITION

PASCAL B., *Pensées*, Éditions France Loisirs, coll. « Les grands écrivains choisis par l'Académie Goncourt », 1986.

BASELINE STUDY

TOURRETTE É., Pensées. *Grandeur et misère de l'homme*, Paris, Éditions Bréal, « Connaissance d'une œuvre » series, 2008.